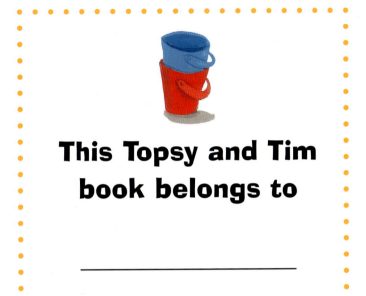

This Topsy and Tim book belongs to

_____

Topsy and Tim
Go on Holiday

By Jean and Gareth Adamson

LADYBIRD BOOKS

UK | USA | Canada | Ireland | Australia
India | New Zealand | South Africa

Ladybird Books is part of the Penguin Random House group of companies
whose addresses can be found at global.penguinrandomhouse.com
www.penguin.co.uk   www.puffin.co.uk   www.ladybird.co.uk

First published by Ladybird Books Ltd, 2017
001

www.topsyandtim.com

Printed in China

A CIP catalogue record for this book is available from the British Library

ISBN: 978–0–241–28255–7

All correspondence to:
Ladybird Books
Penguin Random House Children's
80 Strand, London WC2R 0RL

Early one morning, Dad called, "Come along, tiddlers!
We're ready to start."
Topsy and Tim ran to the car carrying their buckets and spades.
They were going for a holiday at the seaside.

First, they drove to the garage to get the car ready for the journey. Mummy put the petrol in, then Dad checked the tyres.

"The windscreen could do with a wash," said Mummy.
Topsy and Tim fetched the water in their seaside buckets.

"All aboard!" shouted Dad.
Topsy and Tim waved as they drove away.

"Goodbye, everybody!" called Topsy.
"We're going to the seaside!"

They sped along until the town was far behind. Then they had to slow right down behind a big, noisy tractor. Suddenly Tim shouted, "We've left our buckets behind!"

"Never mind," said Mummy. "We'll buy new buckets when we get there."
But Tim began to cry. "I want my old bucket," he sobbed.

"We're all getting hungry," said Mummy.
"Let's stop and have a picnic."

Dad drove down a narrow country lane and
pulled up by a farm gate. "Here's a good
place for a picnic," he said.

Soon it was time to go.

"We must pick up all our litter," said Mummy.

"What shall we put it in?" asked Tim.

Mummy gave them an empty carrier bag for the litter. "We could have put it in our good old seaside buckets," said Topsy.

Dad began to turn the car round. Suddenly, the back dropped down with a bump.

"We've gone into the ditch," said Dad. He looked worried.

"We need help," he said, "and here we are, miles from anywhere."

"I can hear a car," said Topsy.
The sound came nearer and stopped. Then a man
looked over the hedge high above them.
"It's a friendly giant!" shouted Topsy and Tim.

The man wasn't a giant. He was sitting up in his tractor in the field behind the hedge. But he *was* friendly. He fixed a rope from his tractor to their car. Then the tractor tugged the car out of the ditch.
"Thank you!" called Topsy and Tim.

They drove on and soon came to the top of a hill.

"I can see the sea!" shouted Topsy.

"I wish we had our old buckets," said Tim.

Soon, they reached their holiday village.
Dad began to unload their luggage.

"Hello!" he said. "What have I found?"
"Our buckets!" shouted Topsy and Tim.

Topsy and Tim ran straight off to the beach and filled their buckets with seaside sand.

*Now turn the page and help
Topsy and Tim solve a puzzle.*

Topsy and Tim are having a lovely picnic with Mummy and Dad.
Can you spot the five differences between the scenes below?

A Map of
the Village

farm

Topsy and
Tim's house

Kerry
hous

Tony's
house

park

garage

health
centre

post
office

church

primary school

nursery school

police station

Have you read all the Topsy and Tim stories?

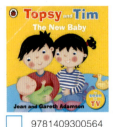 ☐ 9781409300564

 ☐ 9781409300618

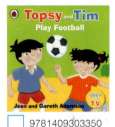 ☐ 9781409300571

 ☐ 9781409303350

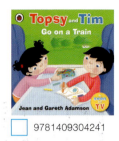 ☐ 9781409304241

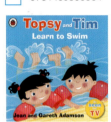 ☐ 9781409300601

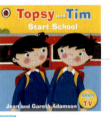 ☐ 9781409300830

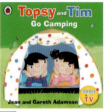 ☐ 9781409303336

 ☐ 9781409304234

 ☐ 9781409300847

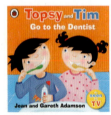 ☐ 9781409300588

 ☐ 9781409303367

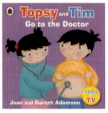 ☐ 9781409303343

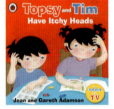 ☐ 9781409307204

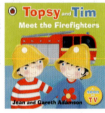 ☐ 9781409307211

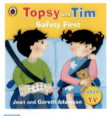 ☐ 9781409308829

 ☐ 9781409308836

 ☐ 9781409309468

 ☐ 9781409309475

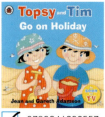 ☐ 9781409311591

 ☐ 9780723292593

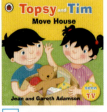 ☐ 9780723292586

 ☐ 9780241189702

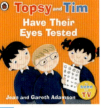 ☐ 9780241282540

 ✓ 9780241282557